Happy Birthday, Sam

Happy Birthday, Sam

by PAT
HUTCHINS

GREENWILLOW BOOKS
A Division of William Morrow
& Company, Inc. – New York

Copyright ©1978 by Pat Hutchins. All rights reserved. No part of this book may be repro-
duced or utilized in any form or by any means, electronic or mechanical, including photo-
copying, recording or by any information storage and retrieval system, without permission
in writing from the Publisher. Inquiries should be addressed to Greenwillow Books,
105 Madison Avenue, New York, N.Y. 10016. Printed in the United States of America.
First Edition   10   9   8   7   6   5   4   3   2   1

Library of Congress Cataloging in Publication Data
Hutchins, Pat (date). Happy birthday, Sam. Summary: Sam's birthday brings a
solution to several of his problems.   [1.   Birthdays—Fiction]   I.   Title.
PZ7.H96165Hap   [E]   78-1295   ISBN 0-688-80160-9   ISBN 0-688-84160-0 lib. bdg.

For Sam

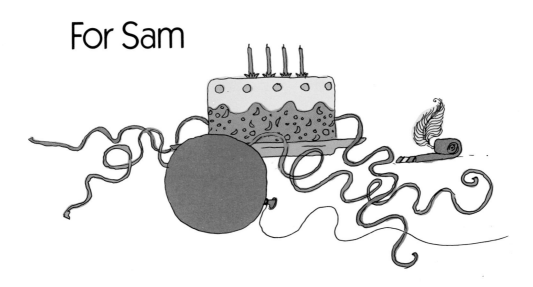

It was Sam's birthday.
He was a whole year older.

He climbed out of bed
to see if he could turn
the light on all by himself,
but he still couldn't reach
the switch.

He went to the wardrobe
to see if he could get
dressed all by himself,
but he still couldn't reach
his clothes.

He ran to the bathroom
to see if he could brush
his teeth all by himself,
but he still couldn't reach
the taps.

So he went downstairs.

"Happy birthday!"
said his mother and father,
and gave Sam a beautiful boat,
but Sam still couldn't reach
the sink to sail it.

"The postman's at the door,"
said Father, but Sam still
couldn't reach the knob
to open it.

"It's from Grandpa!"
said Mother and Father.
"What a nice little chair,
and just the right size."

"Yes," said Sam,
and he took his little chair
up the stairs,

switched on the light
in his bedroom,

took his clothes
out of the wardrobe
and dressed himself,

and went to the bathroom
and brushed his teeth.

Then he took his little
chair downstairs and sailed
his boat in the sink.
"It's the nicest boat ever,"
he said, "and the nicest
little chair."

And when Grandpa arrived for the birthday party, Sam opened the door and let him in. All by himself.